For Paul

Published by Jenny Witchard
Text copyright ©Jenny Witchard 2021
Illustrations copyright ©Jenny Witchard 2021
The right of Jenny Witchard to be identified as the author and illustrator
of this work has been asserted by her in accordance with the
Copyright Designs and Patents Act 1988.

This is my grandson, Stanley, who has a sister called Isla and a cousin whose name is Martha.

When Stanley was little and came to my house for sleepovers, I used to make up stories for him about a boy called Stanley who did very ordinary things, but whenever he shouted, "Look at me," strange, magical things happened and he had some adventures.

On those adventures Stanley became Stan the Man.

Jenny Witchard

Stan the Man

and the

GIANT

SLOTH

By Jenny Witchard

Stanley's a lad you'd all like to meet.
He's the boy that has incredible feet

That take him away on adventures so cool,
You'd wish he was your best friend at school.

The very first time it happened was when
He slid down a big purple slide. It was then,

He found himself in a place full of snow.
But if you've read it, that story you'll know.

The next time it happened was one sunny day
In a pub garden, where Stan went to play
With Isla his sister, 'cause their dad and mum

Said, "We'll just
Sit here,
While you have
Some fun."

The end of the garden was full of big trees
And fantastic flowers with enormous leaves.
And there in the middle - a wide grassy space.
So they went to explore and they started a chase.

They circled a tree
And ran round and round.
They slipped and they slithered
All over the ground.

Then all at once
With a swish......
And a swoosh......

Isla spun round and fell into a bush!

Stan waited for Isla's
Face to appear.
But she just wasn't coming –
That much was quite clear.

So Stanley ran over
And he jumped in too.
He knew that's just what
A big brother should do.

Isla was sitting quite still on the ground.
"Hey Stanley, come closer and see what I found."

So Stanley crawled through
To where Isla sat,
Where the ground was quite brown
And quite dry and quite flat.

Inside was a space
Like a green outdoor cave,
With a tree in the middle.
And so with a wave.....

Up through the leaves
Stanley started to crawl.
Then with a deep breath
He gave a loud call....

It was then the peculiar
Feelings began!
His feet started twitching,
And twirled him about!
The magic was happening,
He couldn't back out!

THEN....!

They swung through the trees
Just like chimpanzees do!!!
Saw monkeys, a snake,
A chameleon too!

Stan the Man bellowed
A loud Tarzan call,
But then lost his grip
And they started to fall!!!

They fell through the trees
And Stan tore his shirt,
And both of them thought,
"This is going to hurt!"

But then something furry and soft broke their fall.
Their long jungle tumble caused no pain at all!

They thought that the voice
Was a fierce jungle man!
But a huge giant Sloth
Was staring at Stan.
They quickly slid off
And slipped on to the ground.
Stan couldn't believe
Who they had just found!

"I'm a huge Sloth admirer, a super Sloth fan.
I'd love to know more about you if I can.

There's hundreds of things
That I'd like to know.
Like what is your name,
And why are you so slow?"

"Sylvester Smith.....is my name," he said.....
"But most of my friends....call me Vesta instead.
I might be quite slow,
...But at least
I am steady.....

Though I'm sure...
That you know
That about me.....
Already."

"I always feel safer....in trees
Off the ground,

And that is where most Sloths......are usually found.
I only climb down......(and this fact is true)
When I need to come down to the ground....for a poo!"

Stan had a think
And then he decided,
For him to slow down
Was a good thing.....provided
That he could be sure
There would be time enough,
To fit into his day
All the important stuff.

"I'd love to hear more,
But you're just a bit slow.
It's getting quite late
And I think we should go.

We'll miss you, but need
To get back where we live.
So thank you for any
Advice you can give...."

"Climb into the hole
In the roots of that tree,"
Said Vesta the Sloth,
"And then you will see
An underground tunnel
That you can walk through.

Just see where it takes you...."

"Goodbye Isla Smila.
Goodbye Stan the Man.
I hope that you've learnt
Something new today Stan."

Isla and Stan said
Goodbye to their friend.
They knew their adventure
Was close to its end.

The children jumped into
The hole Vesta found....

And all became dark as they went underground!
Stan's feet did their thing, as he yelled...

Then all of a sudden,
Hey! What could they see
At the end of the tunnel....?
The garden they'd played in!

The place they should both
Have probably stayed in !

And there was a man
Who looked just like their dad,
And also their mum,
Who was looking quite sad.

"We thought that we'd lost you,
Or you had been hurt,"
Said mum...Then she asked
about Stanley's torn shirt!

"Our adventure was great,"
Stanley said, "But you know?
I've learnt that it's sometimes best to go SLOW."

Look out for the next Stan the Man story coming soon.......

Stan the Man and the Christmas Adventure

Printed in Great Britain
by Amazon

11102982R00022